AT CAKE AND RUN

Bloomsbury Education
An imprint of Bloomsbury Publishing Plc

50 Bedford Square
London
WC1B 3DP
UK

1385 Broadway
New York
NY 10018
USA

www.bloomsbury.com

BLOOMSBURY and the Diana logo are trademarks of Bloomsbury Publishing Plc

First published in 2018

Copyright © Jo Cotterill, 2018
Illustrations copyright © Maria Garcia Borrego, 2018

Jo Cotterill and Maria Garcia Borrego have asserted their rights under the Copyright,
Designs and Patents Act, 1988, to be identified as Author and Illustrator of this work.

A catalogue record for this book is available from the British Library.

ISBN   PB: 978-1-4729-3487-1
         ePub: 978-1-4729-3484-0
         ePDF: 978-1-4729-3486-4

2 4 6 8 10 9 7 5 3 1

Typeset by Integra Software Services Pvt. Ltd.
Printed and bound in China by Leo Paper Products

MIX
Paper
FSC FSC® C020056

This book is produced using paper that is made from wood grown in managed,
sustainable forests. It is natural, renewable and recyclable. The logging and manufacturing
processes conform to the environmental regulations of the country of origin.

To find out more about our authors and books visit www.bloomsbury.com.
Here you will find extracts, author interviews, details of forthcoming
events and the option to sign up for our newsletters.

recommended by

www.catchup.org

Catch Up is a charity which aims to address the problem of underachievement that
has its roots in literacy and numeracy difficulties

EAT CAKE AND RUN

JO COTTERILL

Illustrated by
Maria Garcia Borrego

BLOOMSBURY EDUCATION
AN IMPRINT OF BLOOMSBURY

LONDON OXFORD NEW YORK NEW DELHI SYDNEY

CONTENTS

Chapter One

It was a hot day, and Hani could hear her breath as she jogged around the school running track. Another two laps to go! "I used to enjoy this," she thought to herself.

Running was her thing; it was what she did, what she loved. Or it used to be.

But now? Now it just felt like an effort. One foot in front of the other. Ignore the pain in one ankle. Keep the breath steady.

Hani looked up as she passed her teacher, Mr Okombe. He was looking at his stopwatch and frowning. "Pick it up a bit, Hani!" he called to her.

Hani increased her speed a little. Not too much – she needed to save energy for the last lap. She was so bored!

Running never used to be boring. It used to be fun. She felt happy when she beat her personal best. But what was it all for, really?

By the time she finished, Hani was in a bad mood. Panting, she went over to Mr Okombe and began her cool-down stretches. "Not one of your best today, Hani," he said, making a note of her time on a clipboard. "Any particular reason why?"

Hani shook her head as she bent forward.

"Is that ankle giving you trouble again?" asked Mr Okombe.

"No, not really." A twinge was not 'trouble'. Hani had been running long enough to know when it was time to take notice of a pain. Pain was part of training. Most of the time you just got used to it.

"Not – er – the time of the month?" asked Mr Okombe.

"No!" Hani felt her face heat up. PE teachers had to know **everything**, it seemed! Well, maybe they did when their student was the best runner in the school. Mr Okombe had to know about anything that might affect her performance.

"Well, maybe it's the heat," said Mr Okombe. "It's hot for this time of the year. You're not used to it. If you lived in Ethiopia, every day would be hot." He smiled at her.

Hani tried to smile back. Her grandparents lived in Ethiopia, though Hani had been born right here in England. Everyone knew that Ethiopia produced some of the greatest runners in the world. Most people had even heard of her grandma and her epic marathon running, years before women were supposed to compete. Hani had been named after her, though they'd never met.

Grandma wrote letters sometimes, saying how proud she was that a granddaughter of hers was going to be a runner too.

Mr Okombe was writing something else now. He handed her a slip of paper. "This will get you out of study time twice this week so that you can get some more training in. We don't want you falling behind." Hani's training schedule was pretty full-on. Every Sunday she worked with a national coach. She said it wouldn't be long before Hani was ready to compete at national level – and then maybe even the Olympics!

Hani took the slip. "Oh," she said. "Um…
well, I don't want to get behind on my
homework either."

More training! It was the last thing she
wanted right now.

"Homework can wait," Mr Okombe said.
"Just tell the other teachers I said so." He
winked. "Make sure you do the cool-down
properly, OK?"

Hani sighed as he walked away. Then she
felt bad. He was only doing his best. But
she just couldn't bring herself to care about
running any more.

"Your grandmother would be ashamed of you," she told herself. "You share a name! You know what you have to live up to."

Hani finished her stretches and headed back into school to meet her friends. Maybe they would understand.

Chapter Two

Hani could hear her friends' voices as she reached their dormitory. It was called the Nest because it was one of the cosiest bedrooms at Hopewell High, and it was right at the top of the building.

"Just cut it really short up to the line," Daisy was saying.

"But what if I make a mess of it?" Alice said, sounding panicked.

Hani opened the door and two startled faces turned towards her. Daisy, who had long black hair, was sitting on a chair with her back to Alice. One hand held most of her hair up on top of her head, leaving just the back part hanging down. Alice, blonde and wide-eyed, was holding a large pair of scissors.

"What on earth are you doing?" asked Hani in surprise.

"Daisy wants me to cut half her hair off!"
Alice said. Her hands were trembling.

Daisy made an annoyed noise. "Not **half** of
it, Alice. Honestly, you're such a drama queen.
You're not on stage right **now**, you know. I
just want the back part cut really short – you
know, Hani. Like those celebrities who have it
shaved."

Hani rolled her eyes. Daisy was always
trying to follow the latest trend. Her makeup
collection filled a small suitcase, she had so
much stuff. And as for hair straighteners,
curling tongs, hairspray, gel, dye... well, they
needed a suitcase of their own!

"Daisy, are you insane? It'll take years to grow back," said Hani.

"I know that," said Daisy crossly. "It's my hair, and I'll cut it if I want to. I don't want to fork out loads of money to have it done at a salon. It's an easy enough job."

"I'm really not sure," said Alice, biting her lip.

"Where's Samira?" asked Hani, looking around for the fourth member of their group.

"Studying," said Daisy and Alice at the same time.

Hani nodded. Samira was the most hard-working student in the whole school. "Oh, give the scissors here," she said with a sigh.

Alice handed them over.

"You realise," said Hani, stepping behind Daisy, who looked delighted, "that this is a really stupid idea? And if you get into trouble for this, I had nothing to do with it. Right?"

"Right," agreed Daisy, as Hani carefully cut off all the hair at the back of her neck, right up close to her head. When she'd finished, Daisy let her mass of black waves fall down, completely hiding the fact that there was a bald strip underneath. "I love you, Hani."

"Yeah, I love you too," said Hani. "Idiot. Make sure you get rid of all the hair on the floor before Miss Redmond sees it."

Daisy went to hug her and then stepped back. "Yuck. You're all sweaty."

"Been training," Hani said. "I need a shower."

Daisy sighed. "You three are such high achievers. Alice is going to be a film star, you're going to be Olympic Champion of All Things Running, and Sammy has the biggest brain ever and will someday be prime minister. What'll I be?"

"Married," suggested Alice.

Hani smiled. Daisy was crazy about boys. Her current boyfriend was called Storm, but things hadn't been going well lately, and if history was anything to go by, Daisy would soon have her eye on someone else.

Daisy hit Alice with a pillow, and before long the two of them were whacking each other in a play fight. They could never stay angry with each other for more than five minutes.

Hani watched them for a moment, then sighed and went off to the shower. Olympic Champion of All Things Running?

That's what Daisy thought of her. It was a good dream. But what if you didn't feel it was **your** dream any more?

She got back to the room to find it empty. Daisy and Alice must have gone to the Common Room. Hani sat down on her bed with a sigh. Supper felt like a long time ago, and it would be bedtime soon. She checked the door. No one was around, were they? Quickly, she reached under her bed and pulled out a bag of snacks.

They were supposed to be for emergencies only, but Hani didn't care. Lying on her bed in a towel, she bit into a mini roll. Ahhh, chocolate cake! Chocolate made everything better, everyone knew that.

Hani was on her third cake when the bell rang for bedtime. She just had time to hide the empty wrappers before the other three came into the room. "Chocolate!" said Daisy, pouncing on the bag. "Wow, you've got **all** my favourites. Oh, give me something, I'm starving!"

Hani let them help themselves.

"Chocolate helps your brain," Samira said as she bit into a muffin. "I read about it on the internet."

"Aren't you having one?" Alice asked Hani. She picked up a chocolate bar and held it out. "Go on, you deserve it after all your training."

Hani hesitated. The other girls didn't know she'd already stuffed herself! "Oh, all right," she said, taking the bar and unwrapping it. "Just one."

Sitting there with her friends, feeling the sweet sugary chocolate slide across her tongue and down her throat, Hani felt happy.

This was what life was about, right? Being with friends and sharing nice things?

But later when the other three girls were asleep, Hani lay awake, filled with guilt. FOUR snacks? What was she thinking? That was no good!

All of a sudden, Hani knew she couldn't bear to have that much chocolate in her stomach any more. Quickly and quietly, she got out of bed and went to the bathroom.

Chapter Three

"Cross-country today," Mr Okombe told Hani a week later, handing over a map. "You've done this route a couple of times, but have a look to remind yourself."

Hani looked quickly at the map. She had an excellent sense of direction and she remembered the route. "Just me?"

"No," said Mr Okombe. "Six of you. Ah, here come the others."

Hani was surprised to see Daisy heading towards her along with four other keen runners. "Daisy? What are you doing here?"

"Now, now, that's not very encouraging," Mr Okombe tutted. "We welcome anyone who wants to get fit and healthy, don't we, Hani? Not everyone can be a winner. It's not about being the best. It's about..."

Hani sighed. She'd heard her teacher give this speech many times before. "Yes, I know. Sorry. Hi, Daisy."

Daisy smiled. She was wearing a brand new vest and shorts. "Hi! I thought it was about time I did a bit of exercise."

Hani was amazed. Daisy hated PE lessons!

Mr Okombe led a warm-up and then set them off. "It's not about hitting a time today," he told them. "Just get yourselves round and I'll see you back here."

Hopewell High had a huge sports field but today's route went into nearby woodland. The runners soon separated out, and Hani hung back to keep her friend company. Daisy was puffing like a steam train. "This... is... crazy..." she panted. "Why... do you... do this?"

Hani smiled. "We've hardly started! What are you **really** doing here, Daisy?"

Daisy stopped, one hand on her hip, breathing hard. "I told you, I want to get fit."

Hani just raised her eyebrows.

"Oh, all **right**," said Daisy. "I fancy a lad at the gym in town. Every time I go past, he's on the treadmill in the window. He's so hot, Hani!"

"What about Storm?" asked Hani. Storm and Daisy had been together for a while now, longer than Daisy's other relationships.

Daisy looked sad. "I dunno, Hani. I think he's too clever for me. He's always on about coding and programming and I don't understand a word. It's like he's on another planet. I worry he thinks I'm stupid. He laughs at me sometimes."

"Oh." Hani didn't know what to say. "That sounds really mean."

"But this lad at the gym is just **gorge**," Daisy went on, looking brighter. "And I want to go in and use the treadmill next to him, but I'm soooo unfit! I need to get some practice in before I go. Will you help me?"

Hani laughed. "All right. We need to start at a gentle jog. You mustn't try to do too much too soon."

They two friends jogged on for a bit, but before long Daisy was wheezing again.

"I'm holding you back," she said, between gasps for air. "Look, you go on ahead. I'll walk the rest of it, and do a bit of running when I can. I didn't realise it was going to be this hard!"

"Are you sure?" Hani asked. "I don't want to leave you behind."

"I'll be fine," Daisy said, sinking to her knees. "I'll just have a bit of a sit down, and then I'll set off again. I don't want to be back just yet anyway. Miss Redmond saw my hair earlier, the bit I cut off, and now she's on the war path. Wait for me at the end, OK?"

Hani looked at her. She really, really
didn't want to run the course. But on the
other hand... in her back pocket, she had a
chocolate bar. She could run a bit and then
reward herself with chocolate before speeding
up for the final stretch. Chocolate would give
her energy, wouldn't it?

"All right," she said, and waved goodbye
to Daisy. Then she forced her legs to move.
How far before she could find a spot where
no one would disturb her? Ten minutes later,
she reckoned she was safe. There was no one
around. Hani pulled the chocolate out of her
pocket and unwrapped it, keen to take a bite.

There! That was SO much better. She sank down, her back against a tree, and looked up at the sunlight through the leaves. Maybe this was just a blip. She knew that's what Mr Okombe would say – and her coach on Sundays. Everyone goes through a time when they don't want to train. Everyone finds it hard.

"But I hate it," she thought. "I really hate it. I hate missing out on time with my friends because I have to go running.

"I hate the thud of my feet on the ground over and over and over again. I hate the effort, and the aches and pains, and the sweat. It gives me nothing any more."

The sunlight blurred and Hani realised she was crying. "I'm letting you down, Grandma," she thought. "I can't live up to you..."

"Hani? Hani, what's the matter?" Daisy dropped down next to her, surprising Hani. Daisy put an arm around her. "You're crying – I don't think I've ever seen you cry! Hani, what's going on?"

Hani shook her head, wiping the tears away. "Nothing. It's nothing, I'm fine."

"You're not," Daisy said firmly. "Come on, you can tell me." She spotted the half-eaten chocolate bar. "You should finish this. Chocolate is good for you."

"Not when you eat so much you have to make yourself sick," said Hani quietly.

Daisy stared. "You did what?"

"Oh, Daisy, I'm such a mess," sobbed Hani. "I don't know what to do any more. I don't even know who I am!"

"You're Hani," said Daisy, "the best runner in the school and a future champion."

"What if I'm not?" asked Hani, sniffing. "What if that's not who I want to be?"

Daisy was confused. "Who do you want to be then?"

"I don't know!" Hani cried. "I've always been a runner. It's the Ethiopian blood in me, that's what everyone always said. If I'm not running, who am I? What do I do?"

"What's this about making yourself sick?" asked Daisy.

"I've been eating too much cake and chocolate," Hani confessed. "I know I shouldn't. It's the only thing that comforts me right now. But then I feel guilty for eating too much, and I... well. I throw it up."

Daisy frowned. "You shouldn't do that, you know. It's really bad. You could get an eating disorder."

"I've only done it a few times," Hani added. "It's not like I do it every day."

"That's how it starts," said Daisy. She crossed her legs and looked up at the trees. "That's how it started for Samira, remember?"

"Sammy hasn't got an eating disorder," said Hani.

"No," said Daisy, "but do you remember when we found out she was cutting herself? She said everything had got too much. Hurting herself made it easier to cope. But it started small, not very often. And then she needed it more and more."

"It's just chocolate," Hani said sadly. "And this isn't the same. Sammy's dad makes her work too hard. No one's telling me to do this."

"I bet you hear voices in your head telling you to live up to your grandma," Daisy said, raising her eyebrows.

Hani looked down at the ground.

"Look," Daisy said, "maybe you just don't like running any more. People don't like the same things forever."

"But you said it yourself," said Hani, "I'm Hani, the best runner in the school and a future champion!"

Daisy shook her head. "Well, maybe you're Hani, the something else now."

"The what?" asked Hani.

"Oh, I don't know!" Daisy sounded like she'd run out of patience. "I can't hold your hand and tell you the future, can I?" She got up and brushed herself off. "Come on. I'm no good at being agony aunt. You need Alice for this kind of thing." She reached down to help Hani up. "Don't stress. Stress is bad for you. Chocolate, that's what you..." She stopped. "No, maybe not that."

Hani couldn't help a small smile. "Cheers, Daisy. You're a ray of sunshine."

Daisy gave her a big smile back. "I totally am."

Chapter Four

It was later that evening, and the four friends were together again in the Nest. They were trying to think of other sports that Hani might like more than running.

"What about netball?" suggested Samira.

Hani pulled a face. "No thanks."

"Hockey?" asked Samira.

"Trampoline?" said Alice.

Hani looked horrified. "Did you know you can kill yourself if you fall off one of those things?"

"Fencing," said Daisy. "It's cool and you get a SWORD."

"Not at this school," Hani said, shaking her head.

"Does it have to be sport?" asked Samira. "Maybe you need to find a completely different hobby. Er... playing the piano?"

Hani looked at her as if she were mad. **"Piano**?"

"Maybe not," Samira said.

"What **do** you want to do?" Alice asked.

Hani sighed. "I don't know. Nothing, really. Eat cake."

"And throw it up," added Daisy. "You can't go on doing that. You'll end up with bulimia. And did you know that if you're sick a lot, the acid from your stomach can burn your throat?"

The other three went, "Yuck!"

"That's horrible," said Alice, looking faintly sick herself. Her breath started to get faster, and she put a hand on her chest. "Just the thought of it..."

"Bag!" shouted Daisy. "Bag!" Alice sometimes had panic attacks, and the rest of the girls knew what signs to look for.

Breathing into a paper bag was the only thing that helped calm her down.

Alice said, "Oh, stop it, I'm not about to go into one. Daisy, that was disgusting. You say too much of what's in your head!"

"Well, Hani needs to stop saying no to everything and start saying yes!" Daisy replied.

"I need cake," Hani said sadly.

Alice put her arm around Hani. "Don't worry," she said. "We'll help. You guys have been there for me. We'll be here for you too. That's what friends do."

"Thanks." Hani tried to smile. "Sorry I'm being such a pain."

"What are you going to do about training tomorrow?" asked Samira.

"I suppose I'll have to tell Mr Okombe," Hani said. "I don't think he'll take it very well."

*

He didn't. Mr Okombe stared at her as if Hani had just grown an extra head. "You don't want to train today?"

"I don't want to train at all. Ever," Hani said, in a very small voice. "I don't like it any more."

"But..." Mr Okombe tried to understand. "But you love running."

"I don't. I did, but now I don't." said Hani.

He took a breath. "Hani, this is a natural feeling, all athletes have it every now and then. When it's hot, or raining, or you're tired, you don't feel like getting on the track and—"

"No!" Hani replied. "No, that's not it! I just don't want to run any more. I don't care about winning. It doesn't make me happy."

Mr Okombe smiled at her. "It'll come back. The way you feel right now won't be how you feel tomorrow, I'm sure of it."

Hani felt angry. He wasn't listening to her!

"Take a week off," Mr Okombe went on. "Get your head together. I know it's hard when you have friends and you want to do things with them. But those are the sacrifices a champion has to make."

Hani wanted to scream at him, "I don't want to be a champion!" but she didn't dare.

"I'll tell your Sunday coach." Mr Okombe patted her on the shoulder. "You have great talent, Hani. You were born to run. Don't throw it all away."

*

Hani went to find Daisy, who was in the library. "What did Mr Okombe say?" asked Daisy in a low voice.

"It's no use," Hani whispered back. "He won't let me stop."

"You've got to stand up for yourself more," Daisy said, annoyed. "Honestly, Hani, you're too nice. Just tell him you're giving up, once and for all."

"I tried!" said Hani.

"Well, try harder." Daisy saw her face. "Oh, look, I'm sorry. I know I'm a bit blunt. But you don't get anywhere in this life without going out and getting what you want. No one can **make** you run. What are they going to do, strap rockets to your feet?"

Hani laughed.

The librarian said, "Shhh!"

Daisy smiled at Hani and whispered, "You just have to find something else you want to do, that's all. Find your passion."

Hani nodded. Find her passion. It sounded so simple.

But what if your only passion was eating cake?

Chapter Five

Over the next week, the girls tried hard to find a new passion for Hani. "Horse riding," said Alice.

"I'm allergic," said Hani.

"Badminton," said Daisy.

"Boring," said Hani.

"Cooking," said Samira.

Hani rolled her eyes. "In a boarding school?"

Alice pulled out a leaflet from the local leisure centre. "Swimming?"

Hani hesitated. The other three looked at each other in hope. "It's just going up and down," Hani said, with a sigh. "I like being in the water, but I don't want to swim from one end to the other and back again. That's just like running, only in the water."

"Er... water polo?" asked Daisy, reading the leaflet.

"What even is that?" asked Hani.

"I dunno. Let's go down to the pool and find out."

So on Saturday they got permission to go to the leisure centre. Hani felt nervous. Her friends were so kind. But she felt like she was under pressure to choose, and that made it difficult. She didn't really think she'd like water polo.

"Oh, that's the old timetable," said the woman on the desk. "Sorry. They're not doing polo at this time now; it's the synchro group."

Hani was puzzled. "The what?"

"Synchronised swimming," the receptionist said. She pointed. "You can go and have a look, if you like."

The four girls headed over to the big glass windows that looked out over the swimming pools. The children's pool was full of families, but in another pool was a group of swimmers. They weren't swimming up and down in straight lines.

"Whoa..." breathed Daisy, her face up against the glass. "Look at that!"

The swimmers had formed a circle. At the same time, they all vanished under the water, and eight pairs of legs stuck straight up at the ceiling. One, two, three, four – the legs kicked, and then sank, causing hardly a ripple.

"Wow!" whispered Alice. "How do they do that?"

Hani watched, unable to take her eyes of the synchronised swimmers. They were all girls, wearing identical swimming costumes. She couldn't tell how old they were, but surely they weren't grown-ups? On the side was their coach, speaking instructions into a microphone. Hani could see the wire from it led to a speaker under the water.

The swimmers formed pattern after pattern in the water, and dived under again and again. How did they hold their breath that long?

The swimmers vanished once more under the water. All four watching girls gasped as one of the swimmers suddenly leaped right up into the air, pushed by the rest of them. Hani, Daisy, Alice and Samira clapped loudly. The coach looked over towards the window and smiled at them. Then she said something to the team in the water, and the girls swam to the side, reaching for bottles of water. The coach waved at Hani and the others.

"She's saying we can go in!" Daisy said. "Come on!"

The coach met them on the side of the pool. She was a young woman with an afro. "Hey," she said with a smile. "What did you think?"

Hani burst out, "That was AMAZING!" and the others agreed. "I don't even know how they all did that," Hani went on. "They make it look so easy."

The coach turned to the swimmers, bobbing at the side of the pool. "Hear that? You made it look easy!"

The girls in the pool grinned. "It's so not!" replied one of them, panting.

"Are you girls good at swimming?" asked the coach. "We're always looking for new people to join."

Daisy, Alice and Samira all looked at Hani.

"Oh," said Hani. "Well... um... I wouldn't mind having a go. You know. Just to see."

Her friends cheered. "Go on, Hani!"

The coach smiled and held out her hand for Hani to shake. "I'm Pearl. Go and get your costume on, Hani. Let's see what you can do."

Chapter Six

Daisy, Alice and Samira sat down in the viewing area, excited. "I can't believe she's going to try this out right here and now!" Samira whispered to the other two.

"She's got that look in her eye," Daisy whispered back. "You know, like the look Alice gets when she's about to go on stage."

"Terrified?" Alice asked.

Daisy giggled. "No. Like she's full of energy."

"Like she **used** to look before running a race," Samira agreed.

"When did she last look like that?" Alice wondered.

"Ages ago," said Daisy. She shook her head. "We've been bad friends. How did we not notice sooner?"

"Shhh." Samira nudged her. "She's coming out."

Hani walked out onto the pool side. She was very nervous. She hadn't expected to be doing this! She'd only brought her swimming costume because the girls had thought they might swim together after watching the polo. And now... the eight girls in the water were smiling at her and nodding.

"Don't panic," said Pearl in a kind voice. "You look pretty fit. Do you play a lot of sport?"

Hani swallowed. "I'm... I was... a runner."

Pearl smiled. "Excellent!" she said "Then you'll be used to controlling your breath. Hop into the water and we'll teach you a few moves."

Hani was taught how to float on her back, perfectly straight. "Now lift one leg," Pearl said. "Point your toes to the ceiling." The rest of the synchro team did the same.

Hani tried, and immediately sank under the water. "Keep yourself straight," Pearl advised. Hani tried again, and managed not to sink. "Good!" said Pearl, sounding pleased. "Now try the other leg."

It was very, very hard work. Hani gasped and spluttered as she tried to stop herself sinking. But she was determined to do it somehow.

"Much better!" cried Pearl, and Hani felt really proud of herself.

"What next?" she asked, and the girls on the team laughed.

"How do you feel about being upside down in the water?" asked Pearl with a smile.

Hani's friends watched in delight as she learned how to do a handstand, and then how to push herself up out of the water using just her arms.

By the time the session was over, Hani was exhausted but smiling wider than she had for months. "That was amazing!" she said to Pearl as she got out. "Can I come again next week?"

"Three times a week," Pearl said. She put her head on one side. "Did you say you were at Hopewell High? Will you get permission to come and train here three times a week?"

Hani imagined Mr Okombe's face. He would be disappointed she was turning her back on athletics. But he would be pleased she had found a passion for a new sport. "I don't think there'll be a problem," she said.

Hani's friends were waiting in reception for her. "You did AMAZING!" cried Daisy, throwing her arms around Hani. "When you did that thing where you went underwater for ages... I couldn't hold my breath that long!"

"It's all the running," Hani said. "It makes your lungs stronger."

Alice squeezed her hand. "You look like the old Hani. It's good to have you back."

"Thanks." Hani smiled at her.

Samira said, "Hani... do you think your grandmother will mind that you've given up running?"

Hani thought for a moment. "No," she said. "I don't think so. Grandma always says that a love of running comes from inside you. I think she will understand if I now have a love of something different. It's the same passion, just a different sport. And maybe one day she can come and see me."

"Or maybe you could visit her," said Samira. She held up her phone. "I did some searching online. The national synchro team sometimes practises in Africa. If they go to Ethiopia or somewhere that isn't too far away from your grandma, you might get to see her."

Hani felt very, very happy. She linked arms with her friends as they walked out into the sunshine. "I have the best friends any girl could have," she said. "How can I thank you?"

"Well…" said Daisy slowly, "you could give us some of that cake and chocolate you've been hiding under your bed…"

Alice looked shocked. "Daisy!" she said. "You shouldn't say that!"

Hani laughed. "It's OK. Tell you what, Daisy – you guys can have ALL of it. I don't want it."

"Not even one?" asked Samira.

"All right," said Hani, with a smile. "Just the one."

Bonus Bits!

WHAT NEXT?

Have a think about these questions after reading this story:

- Why do you think Hani got fed up with running?
- Do you think Hani felt happy with the pressure that she felt from running?
- Would you like to try a different sport or hobby? If so, why don't you pluck up the courage to have a go – like Hani you might really enjoy it!

If you enjoyed reading this story and haven't already read *Hopewell High – Like and Share*, grab yourself a copy and curl up somewhere to read it!

INTERESTING SPORTS

In the story Hani finds out about synchronized swimming… but that's quite common compared to these other unusual sports!

- Oil Wrestling – Events are held all around the world but one of the oldest competitions is in Turkey in June each year. The contestants are covered in olive oil and have to try to wrestle each other to the ground!

- Bed Racing – This sport takes place in the North Yorkshire town of Knaresborough. Each team of five people has to provide and decorate their own bed. The bed has wheels but also needs to be able to float. The contestants take part in a 5km run to a river that they have to cross.

- Extreme Ironing – This involves the contestants (known as 'ironists') taking their ironing board, unplugged iron and wrinkly clothes to extreme places (e.g. mountain tops) and photographing themselves ironing.

WHAT IS BULIMIA?

Bulimia is an eating disorder where people binge eat and then feel guilty or depressed about having eaten so much. They then want to get rid of the food and so make themselves sick or use laxatives to go to the toilet. People with this condition often keep it secret because they feel like they have to make themselves sick to stay in control.

WHERE TO GET HELP

Hani used to love running but she feels pressure to live up to her grandmother and struggles to cope with her feelings about this. She uses food to try to feel better but then overeats, and feels worse.

If you have concerns and worries about things, there are people outside of your immediate family and friends who can help.

www.youngminds.org.uk

This website is full of useful information about different conditions as well as ways to help yourself and others. There are lots of useful links to organisations that can help you.

Childline

Childline is a free, 24-hour counselling service for everyone under 18. Childline says, "You can talk to us about anything. No problem is too big or too small. We're on the phone and online. However you choose to contact us, you're in control. It's free, confidential and you don't have to give your name if you don't want to."

www.childline.org.uk / telephone: 0800 1111

Mind

Mind is a charity for people with mental health problems. It can provide help and information if you or someone you know is making themselves sick, like Hani. It is for adults and children.

www.mind.org.uk / telephone: 0300 123 3393 / text: 86463